What If Nobody Forgave
and Other Stories of Principle

Collected and edited by Colleen M. McDonald

Boston
Skinner House Books

Published by Skinner House Books, an imprint of the Unitarian Universalist Association, 25 Beacon Street, Boston, MA 02108-2800.

Cover design and text illustrations by Sue Charles.
Text design by Suzanne Morgan.

Printed in Canada.

ISBN 1-55896-386-3

05 04 03 02 01 00 99
10 9 8 7 6 5 4 3 2 1

What if nobody Forgave, and other stories of principle / edited by Colleen M. McDonald.
        p.   cm.
        Includes bibliographical references.
        ISBN 1-55896-386-3 (pbk. : alk. paper)
        1. Unitarian Universalists—Education. 2. Religious education of children.
    3. Storytelling in Christian education. I. McDonald, Colleen
        BX9819.W48   1999
        268'.89132—dc21   99-30341
                                                                                    CIP

Table of Contents

Preface

From Buddha to Jesus to the Sufi masters of Hinduism, spiritual teachers from various religious traditions have used stories to convey basic messages about truth and right living. The thirteen tales gathered here affirm three ethical principles that are central to the Unitarian Universalist faith. They promote:

the inherent worth and dignity of every person
(each and every person is important);

a free and responsible search for truth and meaning
(everyone must be free to search for what is true and right in life);

the goal of world community, with peace, liberty, and justice for all
(it is our responsibility to work for a peaceful, fair, and free world).

These collected pieces are chosen for their potential to engage both children and adults in shared worship or educational experiences. Supplementary resources have been included to enhance the usefulness of the individual stories as teaching aids; follow-up questions for discussion, a variety of activities designed to appeal to a range of learning styles, and a short list of other tales on a similar theme are offered to extend and enrich the experience of reading or hearing each story.

In these pages you will find a resource for intergenerational worship, children's chapel, summer religious education and camp programming, home schooling, and family story time.

It is our hope that these Stories of Principle will challenge, inform, and inspire Unitarian Universalists of all ages, as well as appeal to a larger audience of others in sympathy with our core values.

Telling Stories

The stories in this book were created to be presented in front of an audience. In this context, telling the story is usually more effective than simply reading it aloud.

Storytelling is a skill that can be developed and improved with practice. It is helpful to have a fairly good memory and imagination, as well as an affinity for the spotlight, but a storyteller's main asset is an enthusiasm about the stories and a passion for sharing them with others.

There are various strategies that enhance storytelling. Notes at the end of several of the stories recommend specific techniques, including puppetry, audience participation, and the incorporation of music.

Here are some general tips on how to be a good storyteller:

- Develop your skills with "natural" storytelling experiences in which you relate your own experience. Choose a memorable and/or dramatic moment from the everyday—the first time you met your spouse, the day you became a parent, an outdoor adventure, a mistake or a triumph— and play it back in your mind as though you are watching a film. Get in touch with sensory details. Recall your feelings. Then tell your story to a partner, vividly and with emotion. Speak in the first person and the present tense, inviting the listener to *experience* the event rather than merely hear about it.

- When presenting someone else's story, don't be concerned with memorizing every detail and repeating the whole thing perfectly, word for word.

  Storytelling encompasses a degree of license, inviting you to make the story your own; tell it from *your* point of view, and, if necessary, adapt it for your particular audience. You may want to condense the story to fit into a given time frame, omit or change something insignificant (perhaps a character's name) in order to facilitate memorization, or add your own slant in order to heighten the drama or bring out the message. Of course, you will want to be careful about maintaining the accuracy of any story you offer as factual, and if you make any substantial changes to someone else's story, it is appropriate to communicate to your audience that you have adapted the original.

- When possible, tell the story in the first person (even if it isn't yours), offering a brief introduction that identifies the character or perspective you are about to represent. This approach conveys an immediacy that makes the story more "real." (Don't be surprised if your audience— forgetting your initial disclaimer—is fooled into thinking the story represents something that really happened to you!)

- Work at using your voice as effectively as possible. Change it as you speak for different characters. Adjust your tone to go loud and soft.

    If a character sings, incorporate a melody rather than simply speaking the words. Tape record yourself telling the story and then listen for energy and variety. You may need to turn up the emotion or ham it up a little in order for your voice to convey your true passion and enthusiasm.

- Practice, practice, practice. Tell a story to yourself over and over again before sharing it with an audience. Don't memorize by rote-let the story come alive and "happen" to you—let it become part of your own experience. Then when it's time to go "on stage," relax. Good stories, well-rehearsed, almost tell themselves!

Unitarian Universalism is a liberal, creedless religion which affirms and promotes:

- the inherent worth and dignity of every person;
- justice, equity, and compassion in human relations;
- acceptance of one another and encouragement to spiritual growth in our congregations;
- a free and responsible search for truth and meaning;
- the right of conscience and the use of the democratic process within our congregations and in society at large;
- the goal of world community, with peace, liberty, and justice for all;
- respect for the interdependent web of all existence of which we are a part.

For more information about Unitarian Universalism, contact the congregation nearest you, or write to the Unitarian Universalist Association, 25 Beacon St., Boston, MA 02108. You can also visit our Web site at http://www.uua.org.

How's *That* for Being Different?

by Joseph Zulawski

There was a little dragon. His mother was a good mom and was proud of him. But the little dragon couldn't shoot fire when he opened his mouth, as other dragons, young or old, could.

Everyone said, "He's *different*." His mother would nod and smile hopefully as she said, "But he tries. He'll learn."

As the little dragon was growing up, other dragons would shake their heads and say, "He's *different*." Sometimes they'd even laugh at him. His mother would quietly murmur, "But he does try." Yes, he did try, but he never could blow even a tiny flame. All he could manage was to throw some small sparks. The other little dragons started to call him "Sparkie." He knew this nickname was a put-down, and it saddened him. He would go off to a nearby cave and hide between meals.

"Something's got to be done with him—he's *different*," the dragons said. "He *is* different," remarked a wise old dragon, "but let's wait awhile and see what happens."

Nothing happened. Sparkie just could not throw flames when he opened his mouth, as other dragons could.

Much later, an unusual thing did occur, but only Sparkie knew of it. One night when he was in his dark cave, while he was throwing his miserable sparks, he found he could do something else with them that no one else could.

By now the other dragons' patience was at an end. They said, "He just doesn't fit in. He doesn't have the ability to throw even a little flame when he opens his mouth." They called Sparkie to a Family Council and spoke to him sternly. "You're different—you're not like us."

"But I can do *this*," Sparkie replied. He opened his mouth and sparks flew out; they were dancing sparks that suddenly froze and then began to change form, each in its own shape. "What's that?" Everyone was shocked. But his mother said in awe, "He's forming an alphabet." "Yes he is," one of the older dragons said quietly.

Sparkie allowed the dancing sparks to float around the alphabet like a frame of fireflies. Next, he let one of the fireflies pull a letter out of the line and set it down below, in a line of its own. First there was an *E*, then an *X*, followed by a *T*; the letters danced and wiggled next to each other like dancers in a chorus line. Sparkie's demonstration was gaining speed; quickly followed *R, A, O, R, D, I, N, A, R, Y.*

"It's a word!" one of the elder dragons yelled in astonishment.

Sparkie threw out three more letters so that the line read, "EXTRAORDINARY I AM." The other dragons looked at each other in astonishment. "A whole sentence." They shook their heads in amazement. "Yes, he's *different*," someone said. "In fact, he's *extraordinary!*"

His mother smiled and said, "Yes, he's different."

Some questions for you to think about

? What is the moral or lesson of this story?

? Is it good or bad to be "different"? Why?

? In what way(s) does Sparkie remind you of yourself and/or someone you know?

? If you were going to give Sparkie another name, what would it be? Why?

Some things for you to do

★ Write and illustrate a comic strip showing the main events of the story.

★ Brainstorm as many words as you can think of that are similar in meaning to "different" and "extraordinary." Use them to make a poem or collage.

★ Starting at the part of the story that says, "Nothing happened. Sparkie just could not throw flames when he opened his mouth like other dragons could," make up another ending that you could act out with others, or with puppets.

★ Make a picture or sculpture of one of the dragons in the story.

★ Interview, read about, or write about a real person who is/was extraordinary in some way.

Other stories you might like

Eggbert: The Slightly Cracked Egg by Tom Ross
A Porcupine Named Fluffy by Helen Lester
Elmer by David McKee
The Girl Who Loved Caterpillars by Jean Merrill
The Cow That Went OINK by Bernard Most

If Christmas Eve Happened Today

by Shannon Bernard

We have heard about a birth on Christmas Eve, as the old story is told—something that happened many, many years ago. But what if such a child were born today? The story might go something like this:

Imagine that your parents are quite young, and they don't have much money.

Your mom is very pregnant with you, and your folks are excited about having a baby. But they get a notice that they will have to drive all the way into New York City[1] to pay their taxes. The trip will not be easy, with your mom so pregnant, and your family's old car that is a bit of a clinker.

It's late afternoon, and already dark, when they start out. There's some ice on the windshield, and the heater in the car doesn't work well. [2]

Suddenly, as your dad is driving on the expressway,[3] your mom says, "Oh my, the baby is coming!" Your dad looks around. They're not in a great neighborhood, but up ahead he sees a star—a Texaco star—and he drives off the expressway, following the light of the star to the gas station.

The owner of the gas station says, "We don't have any place for a baby," but when he sees how scared your parents are, he piles clean rags in a corner and yells for his sister, who is in the back room. Her name is Maria Shepherd.

And you are born.[4]

Maria calls next door for all her children, the little Shepherds.[5] They come in, excited to see a baby. They bring toys they love, and they give them to you as your first presents.

All of a sudden, there is a roar outside. Everybody looks around, and in walk three Hell's Angels on Harleys.[6] They come looking for the service station attendant and instead see your mom and your dad, and you, newly born. One of them takes off his leather jacket to cover you. Another puts a shiny ring of keys down for you to play with. The third looks at your dad's car, shakes his head, and gives your father some money.

The star over the gas station shines. Christmas music can be heard on the radio.[7]

The miracle of the Christmas story is not about angels or even stars. It's not about where or how you were born. The miracle is that you *were* born, that *each* of us was born.

Each night a child is born is a holy night.[8]

This story was written for a live audience and intended to have musical accompaniment; the musical inserts are noted, for those who wish to share this story with a group. The author suggests that a keyboard player or choral group offer a few bars of the specified Christmas carol at the designated spots.

1. In telling this story, you may want to name another large city closer to where you live.
2. Musical insert: *O Little Town of Bethlehem.*
3. In telling this story, you may want to name a specific expressway closer to where you live.
4. Musical insert: *Go Tell It on the Mountain*
5. Musical insert: *The First Noel*
6. Musical insert: *We Three Kings*
7. Musical insert: *Silent Night*
8. Musical insert: *Joy to the World* (sung to its conclusion).

Some questions for you to think about

? How would you explain the meaning of "each night a child is born is a holy night"?

? How can you finish these sentences?
   a) I am glad I was born because. . . .
   b) I am glad [person's name] was born because. . . .
   c) Others are glad I was born because. . . .

? What advice would you give the parents in this story (or any parents) about how to be a good mom or dad? What do children need to grow up healthy and happy?

? What makes a person important? What makes a person valuable?

? What are miracles? Name some.

Some things for you to do

★ Pretend you are one of the people in the story, and retell the story as it happened to *you*. If you are sharing this story with a group, imagine you are a TV reporter; interview various people who were there (for example, the gas station owner, Maria Shepherd, or one of the Hell's Angels) and ask them about what happened there on Christmas Eve.

★ Draw or construct a "manger scene" for this story, showing the gas station and the different people. (One suggestion: For the people, draw the figures, cut them out, and glue them onto toilet paper tubes.)

★ Make a poster collage on the theme, "Every night a child is born is a holy night." Write the words on a large piece of paper. Glue on pictures of babies and children from magazines, catalogs, and shopping ads. Find pictures that show children's differences as well as similarities.

★ Rewrite a Christmas carol, using the tune but changing the words to tell the story of how you came into your family, or to celebrate the birthday of someone else who is special.

★ Plan an "Unbirthday" celebration, real or imaginary, for someone who is special to you. Think up real or imaginary gifts you could give, refreshments you'd like to serve, and activities you could share. Pick one thing you can actually do with or for your special person and then let her/him know what else you dreamed up, making sure to let her/him know why you think s/he's special.

Other stories you might like

Whoever You Are by Mem Fox
When Joel Comes Home by Susi Fowler
On the Day You Were Born by Debra Frazier
Welcoming Babies by Margy Burns Knight
When You Were a Baby by Deborah Shaw Lewis

Give the Ball to Peetie

by Gary Smith

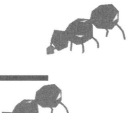

My friend Barry coaches a boys' basketball team, the Campbell Cougars. Last weekend they played the TriCity Tigers at the YMCA. When I asked him how the game went, Barry got this big grin on his face. But then he said, "We lost." "You lost?" I asked. "So why are you so happy about it?" This is what he told me:

TriCity probably has the best team in our league—the best defense, the best shooters, and the best rebounders. We knew they were going to be quite a challenge for us, but we were up for it. I could see that everyone on my team was improving with every game we played—everyone, that is, except for Peetie.

Now there's a rule in the Y league that each boy on the team must play at least one quarter in every game—to give everyone a chance to play. But I hadn't given Peetie a chance to play all season—I'd kept him on the bench; word had gotten out, though, that this was against the rules and that he ought to play.

Our game against the TriCity Tigers was well under way when I decided I'd better follow the rules and send Peetie in—but not yet. The contest was hard fought. As the third quarter wound down, the Tigers were ahead, but my Cougars were running up and down the floor, shooting, rebounding, and blocking as best they could. Finally, I took a deep breath, and then I tapped Peetie on the shoulder. He waited at the scorer's table for a break in the action, the horn signaling that he could go in as a sub. But when he got into the game he could barely run. When he tried to run too fast, he fell down. Peetie had a mental disability and serious problems with coordination; soon it was obvious to everyone why I had kept him out.

But the game continued, as though the Tigers had five players and my Cougars four. Our team would thunder up and down the floor, and no sooner would Peetie get to one end than the boys would rush past him to the other end; he'd turn around and try to catch up with them, all the time watching the game with a big smile on his face, clapping his hands with the crowd.

And then it happened. Someone passed the ball to Peetie. And at that moment, it was as if time had stopped. Peetie just held the ball, and no one else moved. The referees didn't blow their whistles. The TriCity Tigers, who always had their arms up to block a shot, put their arms down. And Peetie, holding the ball as if he really didn't know he had it, started to move toward the basket. No one else took another step. The crowd was silent.

Peetie walked several steps toward the basket and then realized he was supposed to dribble the ball. He dribbled with two hands, because he couldn't dribble with one like you're supposed to. Finally he shot toward the basket; it even missed the backboard.

The moment Peetie let go of the ball, the game continued just as it had before. The two teams fought for the rebound, the Tigers came up with the ball, the two teams thundered back down the length of the floor, and TriCity got another basket. After that, when it was the Cougars' turn to take the ball, someone in the crowd yelled, "Give the ball to Peetie!" And so Peetie got the ball again, and once more everything stopped. Peetie, traveling, double dribbling, holding the ball too long, took a shot. This happened four times, and on the fourth try, Peetie made a basket.

The crowd went wild. Peetie went back to the bench, and the gang lifted him up on their shoulders. The final buzzer sounded. Though our team had lost, we all felt like winners. Peetie was the hero of the game.

Some questions for you to think about

? Is the rule that everyone should get a chance to play a fair rule? Why, or why not?

? How might Peetie benefit from being on a team like this? What could his teammates gain from having him on the team?

? What does it mean to lose a game and still be a "winner"?

? What experience(s) have you had with people who have disabilities? Why do other people sometimes feel uncomfortable around people with a disability?

? What kind of disabilities do *you* have—what are some things you can't do as well as many other people you know?

Some things for you to do

★ Create a cooperative game with a basketball (or some other ball) that someone like Peetie could enjoy with a group without being well coordinated.

★ Look through magazines and newspaper ads for pictures of people with disabilities enjoying everyday activities. Write a letter of appreciation to a publisher or business that provides these kinds of pictures.

★ With your class, family, or some other group, make a poster: On a large piece of posterboard or mural paper, write, "Each and every person is important." On separate slips of paper, write the name of everyone in the group, then have all the group members pick a name. Each person is to add that person's name to the poster, including words and/or pictures to show something special about that person.

★ Think about a problem someone in this story had (for example, the coach not wanting to send Peetie into the game). Write a letter to an advice columnist, as though you were that person. Then write the answer.

★ Pretend you are a member of a cheerleading or pep squad. Make up a cheer, with words and motions, to encourage players, whether they are playing poorly or well.

Other stories you might like

Cleversticks by Bernard Ashley
He's My Brother by Joe Lasker
Why Does That Man Have Such a Big Nose? by Mary Beth Quincey
About Handicaps by Sara Bonnett Stein
Dulcie Dando, Soccer Star by Sue Stops

John

by Liz McMaster

John was a thin, pale boy with brown hair that hung down to his waist; sometimes he tied it up in a pony tail. People meeting John for the first time often thought he was a girl, but that didn't seem to bother him. He was born with cystic fibrosis, so he had a lot more worries than that. Cystic fibrosis is a disease that makes it hard to breathe. The lungs get clogged and have to be cleared from time to time. Being short of breath makes it difficult to be physically active—like playing baseball or hiking. And cystic fibrosis is a disease that has no known cure, at least for now; it can get worse and worse, as people get older, and they can die of it when they are very young.

John couldn't do a lot of things most children do, but he decided to enjoy the things he could do. He collected bears—stuffed bears, carved bears, teddy bears. And he read a lot; he especially liked to read about Unitarian and Universalist history. He wanted to be a Unitarian Universalist minister some day. The people in his church called him their "Minister in Training." John took this vote of confidence very seriously; beginning when he was twelve, he would preach in his church from time to time. When he led the Sunday service, he spoke about what it was like to grow up with an illness that limited the things he could do, and how it was possible to be happy under these conditions. He gave people hope, and he made them glad they had come to hear him. Everyone was happy when John preached.

John joined the Boy Scouts when he was twelve, traveled up the ladder to become an Eagle Scout, and went on to receive the Order of the Arrow, the Boy Scouts' highest achievement. As part of the requirement for Eagle Scout rank, John had to plan a major project. He had seen a Memorial Wall at another Unitarian Universalist church; that's a place on a church's property where people who have died are remembered, sometimes with a plaque that says their name, when they were born, and when they died. John wanted to create a Memorial Wall and garden for his church.

First, he had to go to the leaders of the church to get their approval. Because he was able to explain so clearly what a Memorial Wall is and why he wanted to build one, the church Board enthusiastically said yes to his project. Then John got the help of other adults in the church—an artist to design the wall, a landscaper to plan the garden surrounding the wall, and some workers to actually build the wall and plant the garden. Plaques with the names of church members—and their loved ones—who had died were hung on the wall, and a fountain shaped like a chalice was placed in the center of a small garden of green plants. John included a larger plaque at the end of the wall, displaying a quote by Norman Cousins. The plaque said: "Memory is where the proof of life is stored." John thought these words would comfort people who had lost loved ones; to John, these words meant that people don't just die and become forgotten. Instead, we remember the people who are close to us because they change our lives.

When the Memorial Wall was completed, and the plantings set in, John asked his Boy Scout troop to build a walkway from the church building to the wall—a distance of about 150 feet. Although John, because of his illness, could not dig the dirt or pour the cement, he was with his troop the entire time they were working, encouraging his buddies and thanking them for their help.

John loved the Scouts; he enjoyed earning badges because they helped him learn about a lot of different things: how to build fires, how to camp safely, how to have a good time with friends. But after he received the Order of the Arrow, he discovered something that made him stop and think. He learned that the Boy Scouts of America do not allow people who are gay or people who do not believe in God to be Scouts or Scout leaders. John checked with his Scoutmaster to make sure these rules were real, and then he quit scouting. He quit because, as a Unitarian Universalist, he believed in the worth and dignity of every person—that each and every person is important.

John died just a few weeks before his seventeenth birthday. At his memorial service—which recognized his death and celebrated his life—every seat in the church sanctuary was taken, and there were people standing in the aisles. During the service, John's friends and family talked about how they would remember him. Some of the best speeches of all came from members of John's old Boy Scout troop, who said, "John taught me a lot—he was a good Scout," and, "I hope I can live my life as truthfully as John did."

John was a young person who truly acted on his Unitarian Universalist beliefs. Many who knew him remember John well—not because he died young, but because of the way he used his sixteen years of life—and they try to live as honestly and as joyfully as he did.

Some questions for you to think about

? What does this sentence mean to you: "John couldn't do a lot of things most children do, but he decided to enjoy the things he could do"?

? Which religious beliefs or principles were particularly important to John? How did he act on those beliefs?

? What reasons might (or do) the Boy Scouts give for their rules?

? What do you think about John's decision to quit the Boy Scouts? (Did he do the right thing?) What else might he have done to show he disagreed with the rules?

? How do you feel after hearing (or reading) this story? Explain.

Some things for you to do

★ Write a poem, rap, or song (you can write words to a familiar tune) about a person or pet you've known that has died and how you will remember him or her.

★ Use clay, building blocks, or other materials to design your own memorial wall, garden, or other place of peace and beauty for remembering the dead.

★ An *epitaph*, sometimes found on tombstones, is a short verse, quote, or phrase describing how the person who has died will be remembered. Examples: "No one ever had a better mother," or, "Curious student, Caring teacher, Beautiful Human Being." Write an epitaph for John and for yourself, as you hope to be remembered some day.

★ Find out more about cystic fibrosis or other serious diseases that affect children.

★ Make a booklet of your favorite jokes and riddles, illustrated with drawings and/or magazine pictures. Give it to the pediatrics floor of a local hospital, so that kids like John who are sick (or injured) can enjoy it.

Other stories you might like

Beautiful by Susi Gregg Fowler
Zora Hurston and the Chinaberry Tree by William Miller
Somewhere Today; A Book of Peace by Shelley Moore Thomas
My Two Uncles by Judith Vigna
The Tenth Good Thing About Barney by Judith Viorst

The Test

by Nathan Staples

Growing up as a Unitarian Universalist, I learned how important it was for me to stand up for myself and my beliefs while still respecting the beliefs of others. During my second year of high school, I was really put to the test. I was sixteen and had just transferred to Central Catholic High School. Unlike in my previous school, I had to wear a school uniform and attend a religion class regularly. I had no trouble accepting these rules and respecting the Catholic religion, but many of the other students had a big problem with *my* beliefs.

One of the problems had to do with something called homophobia—fear of and anger and hatred toward people who are gay and lesbian—boys who want to date other boys, and girls who want to date other girls. I wasn't gay myself, but at church youth conferences I had made friends with kids who were. I had learned, without a doubt, that the things I'd heard about gay and lesbian people being weird, different, and bad were just plain wrong and ignorant. So I decided I wouldn't allow my school to say anything rude or unfair about gay and lesbian people without my speaking up about it. I lost some friends because of this, but I felt much better about myself than when I had kept quiet.

On a few days each year, my school allowed students to wear t-shirts and jeans. So I got the bright idea that this would be the perfect time for me to wear one of my sister's t-shirts. The particular shirt I had in mind was black except for the front; on the top, left-hand side, there was a pink triangle (a symbol of support for gay and lesbian rights), with the words, "Boycott Homophobia." That means, don't allow others to treat gay and lesbian people unkindly or unfairly.

The day I wore the t-shirt to school, I made a couple of new friends who agreed with my beliefs and liked the message on the shirt. In fact, one of my teachers even asked me where she could get one. For the most part, the response was what I expected—either hateful or ignorant. All in all though, the day had been going pretty well. Then, during my last class, the teacher saw my shirt, told me that t-shirts about sex were inappropriate, and gave me detention. Needless to say, I was angry, but I calmly tried to explain to her what the message on the shirt *really* meant. She wouldn't listen to me—I felt like I was talking to a brick wall.

I asked the teacher where I could go to try and get the detention changed. After class was over, I made my way to the office of the Dean of Men, who was a counselor for the boys. When I got there, it turned out he had already left for the day (even though it was only three minutes after the last class of the day had ended). Then I went to the Dean of Women's Office, because I didn't want to have to wait another day. Again, I calmly tried to tell her what the shirt was saying, but she acted just like the teacher had. She glanced at the shirt and interrupted me, saying something like, "I am afraid that I agree with your teacher, and it's time for me to leave for the day." I asked if there was anyone else who would talk about this with me. She huffed and said, "If you hurry, you may be able to catch someone in the office." So then I ran down to the office and asked to see someone, but the principal had left, and I was told the vice principal was "too busy" to see me.

The first thing I did when I got home was call one of my youth group friends to tell him what had happened. After listening to my story, he told me he was going to call some people and then phone me back later. When he called back, he told me that I had the support of a group in my town called The Toledo Gay and Lesbian Coalition and that they were going to call me and also tell the newspaper what had happened. The story ended up in most of the papers in Ohio; it was the top story on the news three days in a row, and someone told me it was mentioned on National Public Radio. The vice principal of the school apologized to me, and, after I asked, I was told I could wear the shirt again. The principal also went on the news and apologized, and the school's priest called the whole school down one day for a special sermon about treating people who are lesbian or gay decently, even if being lesbian or gay is wrong. I didn't agree with that second part, but at least he was saying gay and lesbian people *are* people, and at least we were starting to talk about the problem.

After that year I left the school, but I still have friends there. Every time I visit, I am introduced as "the guy who wore that t-shirt," and I am treated as if I had moved a mountain. The school now has more students who are comfortable letting others know that they are gay or lesbian, and the other students have become more accepting.

To this day, my sister still says, "That's the last time I let you borrow my clothes."

Some questions for you to think about

? What kinds of kids do you know who get picked on? Do you know kids who get called "gay," "queer," or "fag"? What do those words mean to you?

? What do you think people mean when they say, "Girls should act like girls, and boys should act like boys"? What do you think of this opinion?

? What does it mean when the youth in the story says, "I lost some friends . . . but I felt much better about myself than when I had kept quiet"?

? Why do you think the narrator decided to wear the t-shirt to school? Was his decision a good one, in your opinion? Why, or why not?

? How might the story have ended differently? (What else could have happened to the narrator? What else might the school have done?) What else could the youth have done to show his beliefs and encourage others to change their attitude?

Some things for you to do

★ Imagine you are going to a school that is thinking about changing its rules about what students may and may not wear to school. Write or make an argument *for* school uniforms; describe the kind of uniform you would require. Then argue the other side—why students should be able to wear what they want to school; include any rules you'd make about what students *couldn't* wear.

★ Imagine a scene at school, at the park, or somewhere else where a kid you know calls another kid a "fag." Role-play the scene several different ways, including what you *might* do and what you think you *should* do.

★ Design a t-shirt that expresses one of your religious beliefs or principles.

★ Identify different feelings in this story. Choose a part of the story that goes with one of the feelings. Draw the scene, or choose others to recreate it in a "freeze" or body sculpture. (Everyone takes a position and then doesn't move.)

★ Some churches and other groups have become known as "Hate Free Zones," where all people are accepted, and everyone can feel safe. What kind of behavior would be unacceptable in a "Hate Free Zone"? What kind of behavior would be expected? What agreements would people need to make with one another? Make a "Hate Free Zone" poster to hang in your bedroom, classroom, church, or other spot; include words and pictures that show what this idea means.

Other stories you might like

Celebrating Families by Rosmarie Hausherr
She's Wearing A Dead Bird On Her Head! by Kathryn Lasky
Pearl Moscowitz's Last Stand by Arthur A. Levine
Gloria Goes to Gay Pride by Leslea Newman

The Dream Machine

by Cherise Wyneken

"Who? Who? Who are you?" Jamie asked as he awoke.

Mama looked around the room as she entered. "Who are you talking to?" she asked.

"I was talking to my dream machine."

"Dream machine? What's that?"

"It's a TV you watch in your sleep."

"What did you see on your dream screen?"

"I saw a giant owl face. A puffy, fat-faced owl. And he stared real hard at me, like he was trying to tell me something. What do you think it means?"

"It was just a dream," said Mama.

"But he looked so hard at me with his big round eyes—it must mean *something*."

Mama fluffed Jamie's pillow and gave him a soft shove off the bed. "It means it's time to get up," she said.

But Jamie wasn't satisfied.

"I dreamed about a giant, puffy owl face," he told his dad at breakfast. "What do you think it means?"

"Means? Well, owls are wise," answered Dad. "Maybe it means you'd better wise up and do what your old dad tells you. But then I don't really *know*."

"Today you get your shots for school," reminded Mama.

"Oh, no-o-o," Jamie groaned. "Do I have to?"

Mama rummaged through her purse and handed Jamie some shiny silver coins. "You're old enough to pay your own fare, now," she said. As they went out the door, Jamie caught a whiff of Mama's yellow roses growing by the sidewalk. *I wish I could stay home*, he thought, looking back.

When they reached the bus stop near the church, they saw the minister getting out of her car.

"Good morning, Reverend Susan," Mama said.

"Good morning," she replied. Then she looked down at Jamie. "And how are *you*, young man?"

"Jamie is upset," Mama explained.

"About what?"

"I dreamed about a giant, puffy owl face," Jamie told her, "and I wonder what it means."

"Means?" asked the minister. "Well, owls are wise. Perhaps it means God has something wise to tell you. But then, I don't really *know*."

"Here comes the bus," Mama said.

Jamie reached into his pocket for the coins. They made a merry, jingly sound. He wished he could keep them there, but when he gave them to the driver, he felt proud. At last, after a long and bouncy ride, Mama and Jamie arrived at the doctor's office.

"And how are *you*, son?" asked Dr. Garcia.

"Jamie has a problem," Mama said.

"A problem? What problem?"

"I dreamed about a giant, puffy owl face," Jamie explained, "and I wonder what it means."

"Means?" asked Dr. Garcia. "Well, owls are wise. Perhaps it means you'd better not eat too many sweets and snacks, or you will grow a fat face too. But then, I don't really *know*."

After all the shots were over, Dr. Garcia's nurse gave Jamie a balloon. Jamie smiled. "Red—my favorite color."

When Jamie got home, he settled on the porch and began to puff at the balloon. He puffed and puffed, and as he puffed, he thought—*No one really knows what my owl dream means.* Then his eyes lit up. *Old Mrs. Murphy has lived forever. She must know everything. I'll go ask her.*

Mrs. Murphy was sitting on her porch next door, enjoying the summer breeze. The wind chimes tinkled cheerfully. The palm fronds made a sizzling sound.

"Hi," said Jamie. Mrs. Murphy looked up. "Hello there, Jamie. How are *you* today?"

"I'm all mixed up about my dream! I dreamed about a giant owl face. It was fat and puffy, and he stared at me. What do you think it means?"

Mrs. Murphy looked at him thoughtfully. Jamie waited for her to explain. How would he know whose answer was right? Then she laughed and said, "I think it means you are a lucky boy to have such a pleasant dream."

"Oh," said Jamie and then he knew the answer. Then he laughed also—"Hoo, hoo, hoo!"

Some questions for you to think about

? Who do you think gave the best answer in the story? Why?

? Where do you go when you're looking for the answer to an important question?

? What important questions do you have now?

? How do you figure out what is true and right?

? What do your dreams tell *you*?

Some things for you to do

★ Make a "Dream Machine" out of recyclables.

★ Use paint or chalk to make a picture about dreams.

★ Tell or write a story that begins like this: "Last night, I had the strangest dream." If you create the story with a group, tell it in a circle, with everyone adding a line or a few sentences.

★ Picture the owl in the story. Get other people's ideas about what it might look like. Alone or with others, draw a picture of the owl, or choose some other materials you can use to make it.

★ Choose a hard question (that can have more than one answer), such as:
   a) What is God?
   b) What's your favorite joke?
   c) Which animal makes the best pet?

Think about how *you* would answer the question. Then ask three or more people to give you *their* answer. After you have heard everyone's answer, figure out whether your own answer has changed.

Other stories you might like

Guess Who My Favorite Person Is by Byrd Baylor

Dream Wolf by Paul Goble

Darkness and the Butterfly by Ann Grifalconi

Dreamcatcher by Audrey Osofsky

You Look Ridiculous by Bernard Waber

Grandmother's Gift

by Colleen M. McDonald

The very first people—our great, great, great, great . . . grandmother and grandfather—came out of the earth, growing out of the soil like a tulip, or a grapevine, or a weeping willow tree. But the earth that they lived on had no plants.

The first woman and man blessed the earth and sang a song of thanksgiving for the gift of life. Then they walked around their home and explored for a time, scrambling up rocks, slipping through sand, splashing in rivers, and heaving themselves toward the sky, on steep mountain cliffs. When they had had enough, they returned to the place where they had been born and settled down. In time, they had children; their children had children; their grandchildren had children . . . and so on.

As more and more babies were born, the land started filling up. Women, men, and children spread farther and farther across the face of the earth, looking for clear space they could call their own, and claiming territory in the east and the west, the north and the south. At that time in the history of the world, no one ever died, and so the earth could only become more crowded.

Finally, when it seemed that the earth was holding almost as many people as could live together in peace, a great council was called, in the place where the first humans had been born. The people decided they needed to stop having children, once the last woman who was currently pregnant gave birth to her baby.

In the months and years that followed, infants became children, children became teens, and teens became adults, until, at last, the feel of a newborn held securely in one's arms became only a memory; the sounds of cooing and babbling, first words, and baby talk faded away; the sight of girls' bodies rounding into womanhood, and boys' faces growing manly whiskers, disappeared because everyone on earth had grown up.

Now, remember, at that time, no one ever died, and so the first woman and man were still alive. One day, the woman began thinking aloud. "Life has been wonderful," she said to her husband. "I've climbed to points so high I could almost touch the stars. I've seen more twilights and dawns than I could possibly count. I've rocked and tended my babies, and their babies, and their babies. I'm ready to rest now. Babies. . . ." she continued. "Children. Remember when our home was full of them?" The man nodded. "I miss them!" they both said at once. "Yes," the woman continued, "I'm ready to give up my place on earth, so that more children can come into this world." "Give up your place on earth?" asked the man. "But where would you go?" "I'd go back to where I came from—back into the earth." "And then what? What will happen then?" the man wondered. "I don't know," said the woman. "But the earth is our mother, and I am not afraid."

The woman sent out a call to her children and grandchildren and great grandchildren, who were scattered among the four corners of the earth. She told them what she was planning to do and asked them to come home.

The woman and the man and their many children gathered on the land, at the birth spot where the now-oldest humans had sprung up out of the soil. The family members shared news of what was happening to them now, told stories from their life together, and remembered precious moments, long-buried in forgetfulness. They laughed, and they cried, and they gave thanks for their time together. No one wanted to say goodbye to the woman, but they let her go, and she returned to the earth. And so, death came to the first human being.

Time passed. Nothing seemed to have changed until, one day, someone spotted a thin, green curl springing out of the soil that had received the woman. In the days that followed, the curl grew longer and longer and sprouted more and more greenery. Tiny clumps, like closed fists, appeared, and then opened to display rainbow colors, giving off a gentle perfume. The people had never seen anything like it! The plant bore delicate clusters, shiny and sweet. Humans, who had never before tasted fruit, delighted in this gift. "So this is what comes of dying!" they said. The plant finally withered, but its seeds brought new blossoms and more fruit in the season the people named "spring."

Reassured, more and more people followed the first woman and returned to the earth, making room so that babies were born once again. Children grew up accepting death, knowing their time would come one day, too.

And so death comes to each of us. The earth continues to call our bodies home. Spring still comes . . . and the flowers bloom.

Some questions for you to think about

? How do you feel about death?

? What do you think happens when people die?

? Should people have a say in when and where they die? Why, or why not? If yes, in what circumstances?

? How can you be helpful to someone who is dying?

? What can you do for friends or family after someone close to them has died?

Some things for you to do

★ Find the obituary section of a newspaper and see what kind of information goes into an obituary. Then write "the world's first obituary" for the main character in the story, adding as many details as you can. If you'd like, draw a "photograph" of her.

★ Imagine what the first flower looked like. Use paint or markers and paper to show the design, or make a three-dimensional flower out of craft materials.

★ Find an interesting plant growing indoors or outdoors. Pretend this plant is the world's first plant; imagine you have never seen a plant before, and that words describing plant parts (for example, leaves, flowers) haven't been invented yet. How would you describe this plant? If you want, share this description with someone else and see if that person can guess what you're describing.

★ Illustrate an event in the story (your favorite part of something particularly interesting).

★ Pantomime (act out without words) the following parts of this story or others:

a) The first woman telling her husband she plans to return to the earth

b) The first man hearing this news

c) A family member saying goodbye to the woman

d) Someone discovering the first plant/flower/fruit

If you'd like, share the pantomimes with others who are familiar with the story, and ask them to guess what part of the story you're acting out.

Other stories you might like

The Mountains of Tibet by Mordecai Gerstein

Lifetimes by Bryan Mellonie

Badger's Parting Gifts by Susan Varley

The Great Change by White Deer of Autumn

A Little Jar Labeled "Freedom"

by Cynthia B. Johnson

Once upon a time, long, long ago, there was a Creator who had a hobby of making planets. The Creator took pride in making each one different. One day she looked at a gap in the solar system and said, "I think I'll make a planet to go over there. Let me think . . . how will I make *this* one?" She sat and looked out into the vast reaches of swirling matter and thought long and hard about creating another new planet in her collection. She had a very large closet in which she had rows and rows of shelves, with little jars and envelopes of things.

To begin, she took a large glass jar down from the shelf and started adding ingredients to her planet—a pinch of this, a pinch of that. In went daffodils and puppies and pizza. She added ladybugs and butterflies . . . and fire ants, just to make her planet interesting. She poured in lots of liquid from the jar marked "Oceans and Seas" and from the jar marked "Clear Lakes" and slowly poured in more liquid from a jar labeled "Waterfalls." She smiled and added just a dash from the jar labeled "Mud Puddles." She decided to shake in a sample from all her boxes labeled "Human Beings." She combined people of all sizes and shapes and ages, many colors of skin and hair, many different kinds of noses, and many different interests and skills. Over all the people she sprinkled some powder called "Change," so that the people would change in size and age, interests and skills. "That will make this new planet interesting," she mused to herself. "I'm glad I thought to do this."

She looked in the section of her closet called "Moods and Emotions," and she wondered whether she should add a little or a lot. She started with Love, adding more than two cups, and then, just to make the planet more interesting, she closed her eyes and reached in and took a handful from the "Miscellaneous" jar, where there were bits and pieces of Sadness and Courage, Loneliness and Happiness, Memory and Hope. She shook out some Schools and Universities, where people come together to learn. She shook out some Churches and Temples so that people could come together to remember what is important in life.

She added comfortable shoes and blue jeans, and warm coats and bathing suits. From her section called "Smells," she shook in a pinch of Hyacinths, a pinch of Just Baked Chocolate Chip Cookies, a pinch of Freshly Mowed Grass, and—just to make it interesting-a pinch of Skunk. She amused herself for days and days, designing her new planet. Finally she was almost done. Almost.

There was one more ingredient she wanted to add. She moved jars around looking for one special jar she remembered that she had but that she had never used before. Finally she found it behind a jar called "Kalimavda" (which she *didn't* add, so I have no idea what *that* would have contributed to her new planet!). She carefully lifted down a little jar labeled "Freedom." This time she had to read the label because she didn't remember exactly what was in the jar. The label said, "This compound contains the ability to make choices, to choose one thing instead of another thing. Use cautiously, because the choices made will have consequences." The Creator smiled as she measured out twice the maximum recommended dosage into her glass jar. She said to herself, "This will make it especially interesting."

She held the open jar in her hands, slowly turning it as she looked down into it. A soft chuckle rumbled out of her mouth and into the jar. A tear trickled down her cheek and into the jar also. She leaned over and blew in her warm breath. And then she screwed on the cover and flung the jar away into the star-speckled darkness. It landed just where she intended—about 93 million miles from her favorite Sun. The Creator watched her planet settle into its new home. She thought to herself, "What a nice piece of work! I hope they'll appreciate all the special things I did to make their planet interesting." Then she sat down with a good book, a bowl of popcorn, and some Kalimavda (whatever that is!).

Some questions for you to think about

? What decisions or choices have *you* made that led to something bad happening?

? What other bad things happen in the world as a consequence of people's choices?

? What are some examples of bad decisions that hurt people? What decisions or choices have you made that led to something *good* happening?

? What freedoms or choices should people your age be allowed to have or make? Explain. What freedoms or choices should people your age *not* be allowed to have or make? Why not?

Some things for you to do

★ Create a recipe for Planet Earth. Include a list of ingredients and step-by-step instructions.

★ Using paint, playdough, or recyclables, design your own planet. Give it a name. Describe how it is similar to other planets, and what makes it unique.

★ Write your own myth:
   a) describing how the world came to be; OR
   b) explaining why bad things happen; OR
   c) answering some other question about why something in the world is the way it is.

★ Compose a rap, song (using a familiar melody), or poem about good and/or bad things on earth.

★ Create a magazine/newspaper, radio, or TV ad for Kalimavda. Consider including music and/or a jingle (radio or TV), sound effects (radio), or props (TV).

Other stories you might like

Terrible Things by Eve Bunting (This story may be too scary for younger children.)

Beginnings of Earth and Sky by Sophia Lyon Fahs

The Fire Children; A West African Creation Tale by Eric Madden

Light: The First Seven Days by Sarah Waldman

The Two-Legged Creature; An Otoe Story retold by Anna Lee Walters

The Children's Crusade

by Kate Rohde

"What are we going to do?" Martin Luther King asked his friends. He was worried; it looked like they were going to fail in their mission. Martin Luther King was trying to lead the black people in Birmingham in a struggle to end segregation.

In King's day, segregation meant that black people were not allowed to do the same things or go to the same places as white people: Black people couldn't go to most amusement parks, swimming pools, parks, hotels, or restaurants. They had to go to different schools that weren't as nice as the schools for white kids. They had to use separate drinking fountains, and they could get in big trouble for drinking out of fountains marked for white people. They weren't allowed to use the same bathrooms; many times, there was no bathroom at all that they could use. They weren't allowed to try on clothes before they bought them.

Black people didn't think that was fair; there were white people who agreed with them. But in many, many places, especially in the southern part of the United

States, segregation was the law—and if black people tried to go someplace they weren't supposed to go, they could get arrested, beaten, and even killed.

Many thousands of people were working in the 1950s and 1960s to end segregation. But one spring, Martin Luther King was in one of the largest and strictest segregated cities in the south—Birmingham, Alabama. There he could find only a few people who would help. At night they would have big meetings at a church; they would talk about segregation and ways to change things. Four hundred people would show up for the meeting, but only thirty-five or so would volunteer to protest; and not all of these volunteers would show up the next day for the protest march. Those who did would gather downtown, parade through the streets, carry signs, chant, and sing, sending the message that segregation had to end.

You see, the people were very scared. The sheriff in Birmingham was a man named Bull Connor. And black people didn't know what Bull Connor might do to them if he caught them protesting. Martin Luther King had already been in jail once, and others were afraid to follow him. Besides, they weren't sure protesting would do any good.

So things were bad. Very bad. Martin Luther King had run out of ideas. He was about ready to give up. And then that night, at a meeting, something surprising happened. When King asked who would demonstrate with him and be ready to go to jail, if necessary, a whole group of people stood up, and everyone's mouth dropped wide open. The people who had stood up were children. The adults told them to sit down. Martin Luther King thanked them and told them he appreciated their offer but that he couldn't ask them to go to jail. But they wouldn't sit down. They wanted to help.

That night, Martin Luther King talked with his friends. "What are we going to do?" he asked. "The only volunteers we got were children. We can't have a protest with children!" Everyone nodded, except Jim Bevel. "Wait a minute," said Jim. "If they want to do it, I say bring on the children." "But they are too young!" the others said. Then Jim asked, "Are they too young to go to segregated schools?" "No!" "Are they too young to be kept out of amusement parks?" "No!" "Are they too young to be refused a hamburger in a restaurant?" "No!" said the others. "Then they are not too young to want their freedom." That night, they decided that any child old enough to join a church was old enough to march.

The children heard about this decision and told their friends. When the time came for the march, there were a thousand children, teenagers, and college students. And the sheriff arrested them and put them in jail. The next day even more kids showed up—and some of their parents and relatives too—and even more the next day and the next day. Soon lots of adults joined in. Finally, a thousand children were in jail, and there was no more room for anyone else.

Sheriff Connor had done awful things to try to get the children and the other protesters to turn back. He had turned loose big police dogs and allowed them to bite people. He had turned on fire hoses that were so strong, the force of the water could strip the bark off trees. He had ordered the firemen to point the hoses at the little kids and roll them right down the street. People all over the country and all over the world saw the pictures of the dogs, the fire hoses, and the children, and they were furious.

Now the white people of Birmingham began to worry. All over the world people were saying bad things about their town. Even worse, everyone was afraid to go downtown to shop because of the fire hoses and the dogs. So they decided they might have to change things. A short time later, the black people and the white people of Birmingham made an agreement to desegregate the city and let everyone go to the same places.

Today, when people tell this story, many talk about Martin Luther King. But we should also remember the thousands of brave children and teenagers whose courage defeated Bull Connor and helped end segregation in Birmingham, Alabama and the rest of the United States.

Some questions for you to think about

? Why do you think the adults finally agreed to let the children march?

? Why did Sheriff Connor act the way he did?

? How might your life be different if you had been born of another race?

? How would you define "fairness"?

? What can children do to work for change?

Some things for you to do

★ Choose one of the following scenes to act out (or write the scene as a short play):

a) A meeting at the church; King is trying to convince people to protest, but most are afraid;

b) A child trying to persuade his/her mom to let him/her protest;

c) A policeman bringing news of the children's march to Sheriff Connor.

★ Imagine you are one of the children about to participate in the protest. Write a prayer or page in a diary sharing how you are feeling:

a) the night before the protest;

b) the night after the protest.

★ Check the newspaper for stories about protests and photos of protesters. Where do the people live, and what are the rules or laws they are trying to change?

★ Choose a rule at school, church, home, or elsewhere that you believe is unfair and would like to change. (Think carefully about whether the rule is truly unfair or just a rule you don't like.) What do you think started the rule? Why would some people argue it's a good rule? Why do you think it should be changed? How could you go about trying to change it? Before going ahead with a plan for change, talk over your ideas with a friend or family member and see if s/he thinks you have a good case.

★ Draw a picture or make a poster showing as many different kinds of people as you can think of getting along or working together.

Other stories you might like

White Socks Only by Evelyn Coleman
The Story of Ruby Bridges by Robert Coles
All The Colors of the Earth by Sheila Hamanaka
Happy Birthday, Martin Luther King by Jean Marzollo
The People Who Hugged Trees adapted by Deborah Lee Rose

The Evil Wizard

by Joshua Searle-White

This the story of an Evil Wizard, and of a girl named Esmeralda.

Esmeralda is a pretty normal nine-year-old girl except that, for several years, she has been on adventures all around the world, saving all kinds of people and animals from the clutches of the Evil Wizard. And the Evil Wizard is, well, evil. He is totally and completely mean and rotten. Once he stole a whole forest of animals and put them in cages in a cave underneath the ocean; Esmeralda had to save them. Once the Evil Wizard stole a spaceship and went to the planet of the Hoodoo and tried to start a war there—he tried to get all the yellow-striped Hoodoos to kill the green-striped Hoodoos; Esmeralda had to stop him. And once he went to Shangri-La—a place way up in the Himalayan Mountains, where everybody is happy all the time and does nothing but ride merry-go-rounds and water-ski and eat chocolate; he tried to wreck the fun and make everyone miserable; Esmeralda had to catch him and put him in jail.

Esmeralda had spent a lot of her time chasing the Evil Wizard around the world, into space, under the oceans, up the mountains, and she had caught him every time.

But the Evil Wizard kept coming back. As many times as Esmeralda could stop him from doing terrible things, he kept doing more. As many times as she could put him in jail, he kept breaking out. It was very, very frustrating, but Esmeralda kept doing it because, after all, these creatures and people needed to be saved from him.

Then one day, Esmeralda decided to go on a trip of her own. All her other adventures had started when the Evil Wizard had caused trouble somewhere, and Esmeralda had gone to help the poor victims. But this time was different. This time, she was going on an adventure all by herself. It was a Saturday, and she was going to climb to the top of a mountain—a mountain she had wanted to climb for a long time. And she was going to do it on her own. She got her backpack, her magic hat, her binoculars, some food, and some extra socks, and she headed off along the trail.

As she walked along, she was enjoying the smells and the sun and the leaves on this summer day. But she hadn't been walking for ten minutes when whom should she see, sitting on the path ahead of her, but (you guessed it) the Evil Wizard, dressed in his gloomy robe, grinning at her. "What is *he* doing here?" she said to herself. "I fight and fight and *fight* this guy, and every time that I think I finally have him put away, he's back again. I can't believe it!" And just as she thought this, the Evil Wizard darted off the path and into the forest. But that wasn't enough for Esmeralda. She began running after him, thinking, "This is it. This time, he is not getting away. I'm going to catch him, and when I do, I'm going to put him where he will *never* come out again. I don't ever want to see his ugly face again."

Esmeralda ran and ran, dodging trees, climbing up hills, jumping over streams, gaining on him, getting closer and closer. Finally, as the Evil Wizard ran around an enormous boulder, Esmeralda climbed on top of it and jumped off, landing right on top of him. He flailed around and tried to escape, but Esmeralda doesn't lift weights for nothing, and he was caught. And Esmeralda thought to herself, "This is *finally* it. I'm going to put him where he will *never* get out." She looked around, and right there, next to this boulder, was a hole in the ground. She dragged the Evil Wizard over to the hole, and *stuffed* him in. Then she looked around and spied a small rock underneath the boulder. She kicked that rock out of the way, and the boulder rolled right over the hole, sealing the Evil Wizard in.

"Phew!" she gasped. "He's trapped now. He's never coming out. And I am FREE!" Esmeralda had turned and walked back to the trail, picked up her backpack, and started off again when she heard a sound behind her. She stopped. Slowly, she turned around . . . and there was the Evil Wizard, on top of a log, staring at her. Esmeralda threw herself onto the ground, pounded her fists, and kicked her feet. "That's impossible! You can't be here," she cried. "How did you manage to escape *again*?" Then she thought, "I shouldn't have just put him in a hole—I should have dropped him off a cliff and let him tumble onto the rocks. I should have taken him to the ocean and let him get eaten by sharks!" And then she stopped herself. "What am I *saying*? I'm starting to sound like him, not me." And then she looked at the Evil Wizard. He looked at the trail, and she looked at her watch. And she realized that she'd spent most of the day trying to conquer the Evil Wizard and nearly forgotten about her climb up the mountain.

Esmeralda thought about that for a minute, and then she realized something else. "Maybe trying to get rid of him isn't the answer. If I wait to go on my adventure until I get rid of him, I might never get *anywhere*. Something has to change." "Okay, Evil Wizard," she called out to him when she'd made her decision. "This is it. I'm going on this journey, and I'm not going to let you take over. I won't let you do anything evil, but I'm not taking off after you just because you decide to show up. This is *my* adventure. If you want to come along, okay, I'll have to deal with you, but you'll also have to deal with *me*."

And Esmeralda took a deep breath, shouldered her backpack, and proceeded up the mountain. And the Evil Wizard—well, he looked around, hopped off his log, and went after her; but *she* continued in the lead.

You may wonder, did Esmeralda make it up the mountain? Well, *that* story will have to wait for another day.

Some questions for you to think about

? Who was your favorite character in the story? How are you like that character? How are you different?

? Why do you think the Evil Wizard was so evil?

? What made Esmeralda so strong and brave?

? Have you ever had a problem that didn't go away, no matter how hard you tried? What was it, and what did you do about it?

? Like Esmeralda climbing the mountain, are there adventures you look forward to having some day?

Some things for you to do

★ Imagine what the Evil Wizard looks like. Create a mask of his face.

★ Make yourself a magic hat like the one Esmeralda took with her on her journey. Describe how it works and what it does.

★ Act out the story, after making up a different ending.

★ Write a story or draw a picture about:
   a) Esmeralda and the Mountain (The Next Chapter)
   b) My Own Adventure

Other stories you might like

Beware the Dragon by Sarah Wilson

"The Half-Boy" from *Old Tales for a New Day* by Sophia Lyon Fahs and Alice Cobb

Miss Fanshawe and the Great Dragon Adventure by Sue Scuillard

A Light in the Darkness

by Alisa B. Barton

When I was a little boy, I loved to play with my father's toy soldiers. I'd set up battles, with guns blazing and artillery thumping. The tanks were my favorites. They were unstoppable, growling over and through everything in their path. One afternoon, as I lay on the floor putting the soldiers into position for another skirmish, my grandfather settled into his favorite chair nearby, leaning forward on his walking stick, his hands folded on top of each other. This was a good sign, for it meant he was in a mood to tell a story. I quickly put the soldiers down and sat cross-legged in front of him, my chin cupped in my hands, to show I was ready to listen (because Grandpa liked good listeners). "You know, Alex," he began in his strong, accented voice, "watching you play with those soldiers started me thinking about the war."

"The war?" I asked, knowing he meant World War II. "What about it, Grandpa?"

"I was remembering the morning I woke up to the sounds of tanks going by in the street, right outside my window," he explained. "The house shook and the windows rattled as they passed. I ran to look out, excited at first, but then I saw that on each one, a flag flew—red, with a white circle, and in the center, a thick black cross, with bent arms. It was the flag of the German army—the Nazis—and as soon as I saw it, I felt a knot in my stomach. We left that day—left the house behind, and everything in it, taking with us only the goods and clothes we could carry. I never looked out that window again."

"Where did you go?" I asked to get him talking again, for my grandfather seemed lost in his memories of that faraway time.

"First to France, but the Nazis came there, too. Finally, to Portugal, where we lived in a camp with other refugees of war. It was hard. I was hungry much of the time. The camp was crowded with people like us, people who'd lost their homes, their countries, almost everything they had. But it was good in some ways. There was a man there, another refugee, named Hans Deutsch, who showed us how to fight back against the Nazis."

"He gave you guns?" I guessed.

"No; no guns," my grandfather laughed. "Hans was an artist, not a soldier."

"Then how did you fight?" I asked, confused.

"When the Nazis rolled through my town with their tanks, Alex, they took away more than my home and the things my family owned. They also took away my spirit. Those tanks were so huge and powerful. I couldn't imagine how to resist their strength, but Mr. Deutsch showed me I could do *something*. I couldn't stop the Nazis from destroying things, from destroying people's lives, but I could help rebuild those lives."

"But how?" I demanded. "You said you had nothing."

"What you say is true," he answered softly, pausing as he tried to find the right words. "We had nothing you could touch or hold. And yet we discovered

76

we each had tools, gifts I liked to call them, that we could share. Take Mr. Deutsch. He was an artist—the Nazis couldn't take *that* away from him—and he was able to use that gift to help others whose lives the Nazis had destroyed. In doing that, he helped defeat the Nazis."

I could feel myself scowling, as my brain worked hard to understand. Grandpa looked at me and chuckled. "You see, people from all over Europe were trying to escape the Nazis. They spoke many different languages, and the people who ran the refugee camp, the Unitarian Service Committee, needed some way to let people know that, no matter what language they spoke, here was a place of safety. They asked Mr. Deutsch to create a symbol for them, something that needed no words to be understood."

"Like when you saw the swastikas on the tanks, you immediately knew it was Nazis and that you were in danger," I interrupted excitedly. "The Unitarian Service Committee needed a symbol like that—powerful, but in a good way."

"Exactly!" my grandfather exclaimed. "I'm glad you understand how important it was. And so, Mr. Deutsch designed it for them. The symbol was a flame inside a container shaped like a cup, and it was called the Flaming Chalice. Mr. Deutsch imagined the cup to be filled with holy oil, which stood for sacrifice to those in need."

"What do you mean, 'sacrifice to those in need?'"

"Well," my grandfather explained, "even though he had never seen a Unitarian church, or heard a Unitarian sermon, Mr. Deutsch understood that ours is a religion that asks people to *be* religious by helping others. And the flaming chalice became a beacon of light and strength in those difficult times. People began spreading the word that wherever they saw the symbol—on the side of a truck or the door of a building-help could be found. It still means that today."

"But Grandpa," I reminded him, "that's not all. You said Mr. Deutsch showed *you* how to fight the Nazis."

"That's right, Alex. He showed us how to fight back through his example. In helping others by using his talent as an artist, he reminded us that we all had gifts to offer as well."

"What was yours?"

"Well, though I was a young man at the time, not many years older than you, I was a fair hand with a hammer and saw. My uncle was a master carpenter, and I used to think I might become one. What I'd learned from him, I was able to use in building dormitories at the camp. I also helped build a schoolhouse there—just one room, but a school just the same. But the thing I was *most* proud of helping to build was the place of worship."

"You mean the church?"

"Not exactly. Remember, there were all kinds of people at the camp. They not only spoke many different languages—they also practiced different religions. The Unitarians wanted a place of worship that could be shared by all, where everyone could worship in their own way."

"It must have been kind of plain," I suggested, thinking of my own church with its stained glass windows and fancy organ. [*At this point you may want to substitute details that resemble the appearance of your own church or meeting place.*]

"As a matter of fact, it was beautiful. When people left their homes, even though they were fleeing for their lives and could take only what they could carry, they often brought one special object—a candlestick, a cross—something that meant too much to them to leave behind. Many contributed these precious—I would say, "holy"—possessions to decorate our place of worship. And some offered gifts of painting or needlework. Others shared the gift of music, through singing or playing an instrument they'd been able to bring or to make. Yes, our chapel was quite lovely."

After a moment, my grandfather sighed and stood up. "Well, Alex, you've been very patient with an old man and his memories. I'll leave you to your game now." And he began to leave the room.

"Wait, Grandpa!" I called, jumping up to follow him. "Could you show me how to build things?"

He turned, and reaching for my hand, he laughed. "I thought you'd never ask."

Today the flaming chalice is the symbol not only of the Unitarian Universalist Service Committee but also of the Unitarian Universalist Association. A version of the symbol has been adopted by UU societies all over the world, including Canada and Britain, and lighting the chalice is a part of the worship service in many UU congregations. However, because, as UUs, we believe that all of us look for and define truth in our own ways, there is no official meaning given to the flaming chalice. Each of us may find our own meaning in this symbol.

Some questions for you to think about

? What do you have that is precious to you?

? What gift or gifts do you have that you carry inside yourself and that no one can take away from you?

? What are some ways to "fight back" against bullies without using violence?

? Suppose you were wearing a flaming chalice pin. What would you say to a friend who asked you, "What's that?"

? What are some of the "enemies" of today that destroy people's lives? What are some ways the Service Committee might help?

Some things for you to do

★ Write a haiku entitled, "Flaming Chalice":
    First line, 5 syllables
    Second line, 8 syllables
    Third line, 5 syllables

★ Make your own flaming chalice by using a medium-sized, clay flower pot. Turn the pot upside down and cover the hole with the drainage tray. Using paints or fingernail polish, decorate the pot and tray with words and other symbols that describe the flaming chalice. Place a small, fat candle (a votive candle) on top.

★ Design a symbol for yourself, your family, or your own congregation. Decide: What important things would you like others to know about you? How can you represent these things with simple pictures? What color(s) will help you communicate your meaning? Draw your design on paper. If you'd like, use fabric crayons to put it on a t-shirt.

★ Work by yourself or with others to create a small space of peace and beauty, where you can relax, meditate, think, or pray. Use only a few special objects that you already have with you, that you can find nearby, and/or that you can make quickly and simply. Place them on a table or arrange them on the floor or ground. Sit or stand quietly in your space. Make music, if you feel like it.

★ Write down a family story one of your parents, grandparents, or some other relative has told you. Optional: add pictures and make a book.

Other stories you might like

The Lily Cupboard; A Story of the Holocaust by Shulamith Levey Oppenheim
Peace Begins With You by Katherine Scholes
Let the Celebrations Begin by Margaret Wild
Old Turtle by Douglas Wood

Spite Fences

by Paul Beckel

Not too long ago, on this side of town, four neighbors were living together in peace and harmony. They liked to get together to play, and to sing, and to have a barbecue in their backyards. (They grilled out so often, in fact, that one of the neighbors planted a grill permanently in her backyard.) These friends always liked to eat hamburgers at their barbecues. Some would have cheese on their burgers. Others preferred just lettuce. A few loved to pour on globs of steak sauce. They felt good about the fact that all of them could do their own thing, and everyone could eat their hamburgers any way they wanted.

All was well in the neighborhood until, one day, the neighbor with the grill got a job in another city and had to move away. As they waved goodbye,[1] the remaining friends shed a few tears[2] because they were sure that no one would ever be able to take the place of that friend who'd built the neighborhood grill.

A few days later a new neighbor moved in. The others watched carefully[3] as the new neighbor moved in her things. They were delighted when she came out to the barbecue grill that evening and began to heat up some coals; it looked like she was going to fit right in. But wait a minute—where was the hamburger? The stranger placed something soft and flabby onto the grill and, as it cooked, it gave off an odor that was too unfamiliar to be pleasant. "Pew,"[4] said the other neighbors. Everyone ran into their houses and locked the doors.

The new neighbor soon came around knocking[5] on doors, planning to invite everyone to dinner. But the others pretended they weren't home. They called each other on the phone, and said, "We've got to get rid of that new neighbor, or at least make sure her awful cooking smells[6] don't pollute *our* backyards."

They decided that they would build fences in their backyards, fences so tall that no awful smells[7] would ever reach over them, fences so high that the sunbeams couldn't get into her windows or onto her grass. Maybe—if they were lucky—the new neighbor would move away when her house got dark and her grass turned brown because all the sunlight had been blocked out. Perhaps then the right kind of person would move in.

And so these neighbors put up their fences—fences the size of skyscrapers,[8] which prevented even the tiniest[9] beam of light from squeezing through. Then the neighbors waited to see what would happen. Unfortunately, they could no longer use the barbecue grill in their other neighbor's yard. But at least they didn't have to put up with that strange smell any more.

They'd been in such a hurry to put up the fences, however, that they soon had a number of problems. First of all, the fences were about as attractive as a clump of weeds, and other neighbors on the block started complaining. Second, the fences were so humongous that they were very hard to paint; it really became a pain in the neck[10] to keep them up over the years. Finally, the fences were so heavy that they started to sag[11] after awhile. One day the fences just collapsed with a BOOM.[12] The neighbors cautiously came out of their houses to see what had happened to the new neighbor. "Oh no!" they gasped. "What if she's hurt?"

Well, she wasn't hurt. *She was gone*! Now, they hadn't seen her since the day she moved in, so for all they knew she might have moved out years ago! The neighbors realized that they had gotten what they wanted, but they weren't happy about that. In fact, they were starting to think that they'd made a big mistake.

That's all of the story I know. Help me figure out an ending . . .

This story includes motions you can use to make it more dramatic and give the audience a way of helping you act it out. These movements are noted.

1. Wave your hand.
2. With fingertips, "draw" tears coming down your cheeks.
3. Use your hands to form "spy glasses" around your eyes.
4. Hold your nose.
5. Pretend to knock with your fist.
6. Hold your nose.
7. Hold your nose.
8. Raise your arms high over your head and touch your fingertips together.
9. Bring your thumb and forefinger close together, with a tiny space in between.
10. Rub the back of your neck.
11. Let your head drop onto your chest.
12. Stomp your foot.

Some questions for you to think about

? What else besides building fences could the neighbors have done to solve their problem?

? What have you learned from someone who was/is very different from you in some way (for example, different in religion, race, culture, or age)?

? Do you have a fence around where you live? If so, what is its purpose? In what ways are fences beneficial? How can fences be harmful?

? Like the new neighbor in the story, have you ever felt unwelcome? Where? What did you do about it?

? Would you describe your own neighborhood as friendly or unfriendly? Why?

? What can you do to be friendly to someone new to your neighborhood, class, or other group to which you belong?

Some things for you to do

★ Design a "friendly" or an "unfriendly" fence. Use odds and ends such as: cardboard tubes, popsicle sticks, toothpicks, pipe cleaners, plastic straws, yarn, and fabric. Explain where you might put up such a fence.

★ Find two other people to make a group of three. Figure out three ways in which all of you are alike and three ways in which you are different.

★ Act out the story from the new neighbor's point of view.

★ Draw a picture of the fences in this story.

★ Write a cinquain on one of these subjects: "Fences," "Neighbors," or "Differences":
  1 word: Title (noun)
  2 words: Describing subject/title (adjective)
  3 words: Actions describing the subject (verbs, ending in "ing")
  1 sentence: Description of what you think or how you feel about the subject
  1 word: Repetition of title or a similar word (synonym)

★ Add to the story by writing about what you think might happen next.

Other stories you might like

Paul and Sebastian by Rene Escudie
Old Henry by Stephen Gammel
Billy the Great by Rosa Guy
Chester's Way by Kevin Henkes
Elephant and Crocodile by Max Velthuijs

What If Nobody Forgave?
The Story of Grudgeville

by Barbara Marshman

In a land far away a wise old man, who knew a great deal about people because he traveled from place to place, came to a strange village. In this town all the people were carrying what seemed to be great bundles on their backs. They couldn't look around very well, and they never looked up because of these heavy burdens they all carried.

Puzzled, the wise old man finally stopped a young fellow to ask, "My good man, I am a stranger to your land and am fascinated by these large bundles you all carry about but never seem to put down. What is their purpose?"

"Oh, these," answered the young fellow in a matter-of-fact way. "These are our grudges."

"My," said the wise old man, "that's a lot of grudges to collect at your age!" "Oh, they're not all mine. Most of them were passed down in my family." The young fellow heaved a weary sigh. "See that man over there? I have quite a load of grudges against his family. His great, great grandfather called mine a horse thief when they both wanted to be elected mayor."

The wise man looked around and shook his head sadly. "You all look so unhappy. Is there no way to get rid of these burdens?"

"We've forgotten how," said the young fellow, shifting his load a little. "You see, at first we were proud of our grudges. Tourists came from miles around. But after a few years, Grudgeville became a dreary place. Nobody came. And we had forgotten how to stop it all."

"If you really want to get rid of those grudges," said the wise old man, "I think I know five magic words that will do the trick."

"You do?" asked the fellow hopefully. "That would be a miracle. I'll go and have the mayor call the people of Grudgeville together." And off he went, as fast as his grudges would let him.

You can imagine that the mayor lost no time in calling the people to gather in the village square. She and the wise old man stood on a platform where they could see all the villagers. Many of the townspeople were so bent over with their burdens that they couldn't look up at all.

When they had quieted down, the mayor said, "Good people of Grudgeville, a wonderful thing has happened! A very wise stranger has come into our town. He says he can tell us the magic words to help us get rid of these grudges we have carried for generations. How many of you would like to be able to straighten up, have your grudges disappear, look at the world in a whole new way? Listen to the wise words of our visitor, then, and do as he tells you."

"My friends, these are simple words, yet some people find them hard to say," said the wise stranger. "I think you have the courage to speak them. The trick is that you must say them to each other and truly mean them. The first two are, 'I'm sorry.' Can you say them? Now say them to each other. The other three are, 'I forgive you.' Can you say that? Now say them to each other."

There was a long, silent pause, then a low grumble from the townspeople. First one person, and then another, said the words. Soon they were all saying them to each other—quietly at first and then louder. And then—would you believe it? Just like the wise man predicted, those grudges disappeared like magic! What joy there was in the town. People were heard saying, "Look how those trees have grown!" and "Is that you, Jim? How good to see your face!"

There was dancing in the streets that day, and it wasn't long before they changed the name of the town to Joytown.

This story was developed for use with hand puppets or flannel board. The suggested background is the facade of a town hall, with a sign reading GRUDGEVILLE. The sign should have holes punched in either end, through which pins hold it to the board so it can be turned over at the end, to read JOYTOWN. For the flannel board, cardboard figures can be joined at the waist and held onto the board with folded masking tape.

Some questions for you to think about

? Do you think it's a good idea to make people apologize when they've done something wrong? Why, or why not?

? How can you tell when an apology is real—when the person making it is truly sorry?

? What are some ways, besides apologizing, that you can show someone you're sorry?

? Can you remember a time, not too long ago, when you apologized to someone? What were the circumstances, and how did you feel? When has someone apologized to you? How did you feel then?

? Are you able to forgive a person who has hurt you but isn't willing to apologize? If so, how do you do it?

Some things for you to do

★ Create a dance showing townspeople getting rid of their burdens.

★ Make an "I'm sorry" card for someone to whom you want to apologize.

★ Imagine what a grudge, or a bundle of grudges, looks like. What would you see when you opened the bundle? Use paints, clay, or recyclables to make a grudge or bundle of grudge(s).

★ Along the left-hand side of a piece of paper, spell out "MAGIC WORDS" diagonally. Using "I" as the beginning of the first word, write, "I'm sorry." Use the other letters to spell out other "magic words" we can use to solve a disagreement or make up after a quarrel. Then copy the whole thing onto a larger piece of paper and make a poster by adding pictures.

★ Pretend you are a reporter doing a story about the town that changed its name from "Grudgeville" to "Joytown." Come up with a headline and then write a news story about how this change came to be. Draw a "photo" to go along with the story.

Other stories you might like

Winter Fox by Jennifer Brutschv (This is a painful and powerful story about forgiveness, for older children.)
Even If I Did Something Awful by Barbara Shook Hazen
Dinah's Mad, Bad Wishes by Barbara Joose
Giant John by Arnold Lobel

About the Contributors

Alisa B. Barton is a mother, elementary teacher, and lifelong Unitarian Universalist. She was inspired to research and write "A Light in the Darkness" after the children in her religious education class asked her about the origins of the flaming chalice. Because she enjoys storytelling and finds it effective in teaching, she chose to answer her students' questions by way of this story.

The Reverend Paul Beckel was born in Wadena, Minnesota in 1964. He currently serves as parish minister at SouthWest Unitarian Universalist Church in Strongsville, Ohio. He lives with his wife, Jane Robins Beckel, and has three children: Rick, Ben, and Jonathan.

The Reverend Shannon Bernard was a Unitarian Universalist minister and a storyteller at heart. "If Christmas Happened Today" was inspired by her desire for the children of her church to have access to the basic message of Jesus' birth and for adults and children alike to claim the potential in their own lives. It has grown and changed each year in the retelling. Shannon died of cancer before this book went to press but was delighted at the opportunity to leave this story behind for all of us.

The Reverend Cynthia B. Johnson is minister of First Unitarian Church of Oklahoma City. Before entering the ministry (in midlife), Cynthia was an elementary school teacher, day care director, writer for the development office in a university, teacher of bridge, and, most abidingly, a community volunteer specializing in education and government. Cynthia, who is also a poet, wrote this creation story to accompany a sermon on evil.

The Reverend Barbara Marshman ministered to children for sixty of her eighty-six years of life. She was beloved by them, as she in turn loved and respected them. Along with Charlene Brotman and the Rev. Ann Fields, co-authors, she wrote *Why Do Bad Things Happen?*, *How Can I Know What to Believe?*, *Holidays and Holy Days*, and *The UU Kids Book.*

The Reverend Colleen M. McDonald, the daughter and granddaughter of writers, has enjoyed writing since she was in elementary school. In addition to writing sermons, newsletter columns, and curricula, she likes to write in her journal and compose poems. "Grandmother's Gift" was written for a multigenerational Easter Sunday service at the Unitarian Universalist Church in Rockford, Illinois, where Colleen has been minister of religious education since 1989.

The Reverend Liz McMaster was ordained to the Unitarian Universalist ministry in 1988 and has served churches in North Carolina, Florida, and Colorado. The character of John is based on a member of one of her congregations. Liz hikes, gardens, reads, knits, and loves her granddaughter.

The Reverend Kate Rohde is a Unitarian Universalist minister serving the Unitarian Fellowship of West Chester, in Pennsylvania. She became a Unitarian at the age of seven at a fellowship in Corvallis, Oregon. She has always loved good stories.

Dr. Joshua Searle-White has been telling the story of the Evil Wizard to his children on car trips and at bedtimes for several years. The version in this anthology was written as a retelling of a sermon for a Unitarian Universalist worship service. Josh is a clinical psychologist who teaches at Allegheny College in Meadville, Pennsylvania, where his wife and two daughters are very active in the Unitarian Universalist church. He also tells his stories on a local public radio station, WQLN, in Erie.

The Reverend Gary Smith has been senior minister of the First Parish in Concord, Massachusetts since 1988. He has worked for the Unitarian Universalist Association at its headquarters in Boston, and has served churches in Middletown, Connecticut, and Bangor, Maine. It was in Maine where the story of "Peetie" and the wonderful basketball game actually took place, around 1980, and the oral story arose out of an interfaith minister's storytelling group. David Glusker, a Methodist minister, fashioned the story into words, and Gary wrote it down for his appearance before the Ministerial Fellowship Committee.

Nathan Staples is a lifelong Unitarian Universalist who grew up in the First Unitarian Church of Toledo, Ohio. He is interested in all aspects of Unitarian Universalism, but his passion is youth ministry. Twenty years old when his story was chosen for this anthology, Nathan attends the University of Toledo and plans on attending seminary.

Cherise Wyneken is a freelance writer of poetry, articles, and fiction. She hopes to encourage her readers to seek answers to their questions about life and God, things seen and unseen, and dreams.

Joseph Zulawski is a retired art teacher and professional artist who began losing his sight in 1990. He is a member of the Glenview Unitarian Fellowship and a participant in the Readers and Listeners creative writing group sponsored by the Third Unitarian Church of Chicago. Mary, his wife, uses a computer to produce his work.